Dorrie and The Queen

Martin Waddell

Illustrated by

Scoular Anderson

OXFORD
UNIVERSITY PRESS

OXFORD
UNIVERSITY PRESS

Great Clarendon Street, Oxford OX2 6DP

Oxford University Press is a department of the University of Oxford.
It furthers the University's objective of excellence in research, scholarship,
and education by publishing worldwide in

Oxford   New York

Auckland   Cape Town   Dar es Salaam   Hong Kong   Karachi
Kuala Lumpur   Madrid   Melbourne   Mexico City   Nairobi
New Delhi   Shanghai   Taipei   Toronto

With offices in

Argentina   Austria   Brazil   Chile   Czech Republic   France   Greece
Guatemala   Hungary   Italy   Japan   Poland   Portugal   Singapore
South Korea   Switzerland   Thailand   Turkey   Ukraine   Vietnam

Oxford is a registered trade mark of Oxford University Press
in the UK and in certain other countries

British Library Cataloguing in Publication Data

Data available

ISBN 978-0-19-915178-3

3 5 7 9 10 8 6 4

Mixed Pack (1 of 6 different titles): ISBN 978-0-19-915176-9
Class Pack (6 copies of 6 titles): ISBN 978-0-19-915175-2

Printed in China by Imago

Contents

3 Orley Cottages
Cowhill
Thursday 5th August

Dear Queen,

I think you've been working too hard and you need a day off from your duties.

If you can get away, please visit me and we could play games in my garden.

Yours sincerely,

Your friend,

Doris Bean

Chapter 1

The Queen up a Tree

One day, Doris Bean wrote to the
Queen.

The next day, Doris got tea ready
and sat around for ages. But the Queen
didn't come. So Doris went to check
her Garden Worm Watch, instead. She
was counting worms beneath the big
tree in the garden, when ...

"Psst! Doris," someone hissed from the tree. "I've just escaped from my footman and butler. Is it safe to come down?"

It was the Queen.

"There's only me here, Queen," said Doris.

"Yippee! Let's play!" shouted the Queen. She hopped down from the tree, so she could play games with Doris.

They played Tag
and Hide and Seek
and I-am-the-Queen-of-the-Castle.
(This was one the Queen knew very
well.)

"Hopscotch next!" cried the Queen.
She hadn't played hopscotch for ages,
except by herself in her room, all
alone. No one plays hopscotch with
queens.

Then ...

Right through the hedge came a
tank. Out of the tank jumped the
Queen's footman and butler.

(The one looking grim is the butler.
The one with the wig is the footman.)

"Gotcha, Ma'am!" cried the butler, grabbing the Queen.

"Save me, Doris!" the Queen cried, but the footman was too fast.

He grabbed Doris. He slipped a ball and chain on her leg, so she couldn't move.

"You're a very bold Queen. You've really upset the Queen Mum, running off," the Queen's butler scolded. "You're coming home with us, right this minute!"

"Shan't!" said the Queen, stamping her foot. "I've only been free for an hour."

But the butler grabbed one end of the Queen ...

... and the footman took the other
and they carried the Queen back to the
tank.

The Queen kicked
and shouted
and struggled
and wriggled ...
but she had to go back in the tank.
Doris couldn't help. She was trying
to get the ball and chain off her leg.

KK345269

"We'll be watching you, Doris Bean!" the footman and the butler shouted.

Then the tank went back through the hole it had made in Doris' hedge.

A piece of paper flew out of the tank. It was a note from the Queen.

That's when Doris knew she was in for an adventure!

Chapter 2

The Royal Escape Plan

Doris dropped the ball and chain.

Then she ran over and picked up the Queen's note. It was written on royal note paper.

HM

MEMO

FROM: H M THE QUEEN

TO: DORIS BEAN

SUBJECT: My Royal Escape Plan

Dear Doris,

Come to my castle at sunrise.
Whistle three times. Bring a rope
and a two-seater bike and a disguise
to fit a medium-sized queen.

Yours secretly
Your royal friend,

The Queen

The next morning, before dawn,
Doris crept to the castle.

She'd hidden the bike in the hedge.

Doris whistled, 'God Save the
Queen' three times very softly, just as
the sun rose.

A window opened high up, and out
looked the Queen.

"Chuck up the rope, Doris. I want
to get down!" hissed the Queen.

Doris had brought her toy bow and arrow with her.

She tied the rope to the arrow. There was a sucker on the end of the arrow. Doris knew that the arrow would stick to the wall. Then the Queen could slide down the rope.

went the bow.

went the arrow.

And

It stuck to the wall near the window.

"Well done, Doris!" cried the Queen, hitching up her pyjamas.

The Queen slid down the rope. But the arrow gave way and ...

SPLÅTTTT!

The poor Queen was dumped in the moat.

The Queen's golden pyjamas got wet, but she wasn't hurt. She could swim like a fish. All queens learn to swim when they're on their yachts.

"Let's go!" cried the Queen, bouncing out of the moat.

"Where to?" asked Doris.

"To the seaside!" cried the Queen. "I haven't paddled for ages."

They jumped on to the bike, and tore off down the street.

The Queen had long legs, so she worked the pedals.

"Remember your Highway Code, Queen!" Doris shouted.

Doris dinged the bell to warn people that their Queen was coming.

Ding! Ding! Ding! DING!

"Wow!" cried Doris, looking behind her, but the Queen pedalled furiously on.

The Queen and Doris dumped their bike at the back of the train station.

"Oh well," Doris murmured, "at least no one got hurt!"

Doris bought two day-return tickets
(Super Saver) to the seaside.

The Queen changed into her
disguise. Doris had brought her a pair
of black jeans (medium-size) and a top.
She had also brought a flashy pair of
dark glasses with butterfly wings.

They got on the train.

"Does my disguise work?" asked the
Queen.

"Take the crown off, Queen," Doris advised.

The Queen put her crown on the seat beside her.

When they got off the train, the Queen was very excited.

She saw the sea, and wanted to paddle at once. So they ran down to the beach for a paddle.

They made sandcastles. They fished
for crabs in the rock pools, and then
they walked on the sand for what
seemed like ages and ages.

Then ...

"Queen," Doris asked. "Where's
your crown?"

"Oh, golly," the Queen gasped.
She had left her crown on the train.

Someone had spotted it and got on
the phone to the butler.

He searched the palace, but there
was no sign of the Queen.

Then he found Doris' footprints
down by the moat, and Doris' rope,
and her arrow.

"Doris Bean's at it again. She's stolen the Queen," sighed the butler.

And he ordered the police to start hunting for the Queen and Doris.

Chapter 3

The Hunt for Doris

"Look! That's done it!" said Doris.
They'd come up to the shop to buy an
ice-cream. And that is where Doris
saw the newspaper.

DORIS BEAN STEALS QUEEN!
HUNT FOR MISSING MONARCH!

Doris was upset. Police were
running all over the place searching
for the Queen. What would happen
when they found her?

One thing was for sure.

They were going to be very angry with Doris.

The Queen looked worried. But she was really quite pleased by the fuss.

"One likes to know one is missed," she murmured to Doris.

"You'd better ring home, Queen. Tell them I haven't stolen you," Doris suggested. But the Queen wasn't listening.

She'd seen the funfair.

The Queen tried to walk in without paying, as queens usually do. But the man told her she had to queue with everyone else.

The Queen was really cross, until Doris told her what a queue was. Then she was pleased.

The Queen liked meeting her people, and there were lots of them in the queue. She gossiped a lot with old ladies.

"What shall we do first?" asked the Queen.

"Give ourselves up," said poor
Doris. But the Queen was heading off
for the speedboats.

Doris got drenched. So did the
Queen.

They slid down the slippery dip.

Doris ended up in a pile under
the Queen.

"Now for this one!" cried the Queen.

She dragged Doris on to the Spooky
Ghost Train.

"YAAAAA," yelled the Queen.
"OOO OOOOOH," the Queen
shuddered and shook.

"AAAAAAAAAAA!" screamed the
Queen.

"Let's do that again!" said the
Queen. "One just *adores* being scared!"

"Ring home NOW, Queen," Doris
pleaded.

"Not till one's finished one's fun!"
said the Queen. She had just seen the
dodgems.

"Oh, no, Ma'am!" gasped Doris. (She
remembered the bicycle ride.)

She was too late.

The Queen grabbed the steering
wheel of the red car. It was number
thirteen.

"Buzz off, lady! You've busted my dodgem!" the man told the Queen, when she climbed from the wreckage.

"Don't you dare be rude to your Queen!" said the Queen.

The dodgem man took a sharp look at the Queen. He lifted her glasses up off her nose. He knew it was her. And he ran off to fetch the police.

"Run, Queen!" Doris yelled. "Run, or they'll catch us!"

They got away from the fair, but there were police everywhere.

They were all looking at pictures of Doris.

"I need a disguise," Doris decided.

Chapter 4

The Queen on the Run

Doris bought a huge Mexican hat.
She pulled it down over her ears. Now,
no one could see she was Doris.

Even the Queen didn't know Doris
was Doris, until the hat stopped beside
her and spoke. "Don't tell anyone else
you are Queen, Queen. Even if they
are rude," Doris whispered. "We're on
the run. We've got to be careful."

They went into the cinema. It was a good place to hide. It was dark inside, and no one could see them.

But when they came out, a policeman was asking everyone questions.

He saw a lady in butterfly glasses with a small someone all covered up in a very big hat ... and something about them made him suspicious.

"Beg your pardon, madam, have you seen our Queen?" the policeman asked.

"Yes, I have," said the lady, quick as a flash. "She went that way on a horse, with a girl who was wearing a hat. The hat looked just like the one that my friend is wearing."

"If I catch Doris, we'll split the reward," cried the policeman. He ran off, blowing his whistle like mad.

Then he stopped whistle blowing and stood still, looking puzzled. He thought about what the lady had said. And what had made him suspicious.

The policeman whirled right round. He ran back, shouting, "Stop, Queen and Doris! You're nicked!"

By this time, the Queen and Doris were far, far away.

They were running like mad. They dodged this way ...

... and this way ...

... and that.

"Oh, pardon me!" said the Queen. And this way and that ...

… through the crowd.

"Phew! That was close!" breathed
the Queen, diving into a bus shelter.

Then she hid behind Doris' hat,
hoping she wouldn't be seen.

"We're sunk this time, Queen,"
Doris cried. She was looking at the
poster stuck up on the wall.

"Oh, no!" Doris groaned. "Now I'll
go to prison for stealing the Queen."

Chapter 5

"What Does One Do Now?"

They stayed in the bus shelter.

Doris was afraid to go out, in case she was arrested.

The Queen wasn't much use.

She kept asking, "What does one do now, Doris?"

"I don't know," said Doris. "I'm just about to get arrested."

The Queen thought for a bit. She saw Doris was scared. She wanted to help her.

Then the Queen's face brightened up.

"I *am* the Queen, Doris!" she said. "Queens tell people what to do."

"Stop boasting, Queen!" Doris moped. "I know that already."

"There are some good things about being Queen," said the Queen.

"Like what, Queen?" asked Doris.

"Like ... I'm the boss of all the police, and I own all the prisons!" the Queen said. "That's what queens are for. It comes with the job. The police can't arrest me. I'll just tell them you didn't steal me. No one will argue, because I am the Queen, after all."

"That's all right then," said Doris. "But we ought to go home, before things get worse."

"Don't want to!" pouted the Queen.

"My mum will be cross!" Doris said. "I'm not supposed to go stealing queens."

"Well, okay, Doris!" sighed the Queen. "I'll explain to your mum. I'll call for my car and we'll go home, right now."

And she did, from a telephone outside the post office. Doris kept watch, in case any police came by.

And so Doris rode home in the royal Rolls Royce with the Queen.

Everyone cheered as they drove up to Doris' house.

Then Doris popped out, straight into the arms of her mum.

Next day, a top secret note came for Doris. It was hidden inside a cake from the Queen.

TOP SECRET NOTE
For D. Bean's eyes only

Dear Doris,
One demands to be stolen again. Please arrange it soon.

Yours sincerely,
Your royal friend
The Queen

Now they slip out once a week,
using brand new disguises.

Which one is Doris? Which one is
the Queen?

About the author

I was answering letters sent to me by a school. A little girl wanted to know if I would like to come to tea at her house. Suppose she'd started her letter "Dear Queen" instead of "Dear Martin Waddell"? What might the letter have said?

That kind of supposing often gives me the start of a story ... as it did with Doris Bean.